OtterTwinMagic

by Katherine A Smith

Kasmith

Art & Books

For my nephews.

Books by Katherine A Smith

Children's Books

Otter Twin Magic

Fantasy Novels

The Northnest Saga
Hawkwind's Tale

The Dragonic Voyages
Dragons to Loose
Dragonic Freedom
Dragonic Pride
Dragons to Keep

Otter Twin Magic

by Katherine A Smith

In the deep forests of Northern California lived a family of otters. The father was Gregg. The mother was Valerie. Gregg and Valerie spent their days fishing for delicious, shiny fish to bring to their family, or making their home under the riverbank beautiful and comfy.

1

You were watching the boys *and* you caught *two* fish?

Gregg and Valerie worked hard to take good care of their twin otter boys, Lukas and Jaxon, who spent their days playing in ponds and streams and running through the forests and meadows. Jaxon and Lukas were each other's best friends, as well as being brothers.

One day
they were
exploring
farther from
their home than
they'd ever gone
before, when they
came upon a huge,
towering waterfall.

Wow!

Let's go closer.

The waterfall made a pool
at the bottom. Lukas and Jaxon—
being river otters—weren't afraid
to jump right in. Adult river otters can hold
their breaths for eight minutes. Jaxon and Lukas
couldn't hold theirs that long yet, but they often
practiced with each other to see who could hold his
breath longer.

Jaxon swam over to join him and the two otters moved closer for a better look—but then the thundering water caught them and dragged them under!

Jaxon and Lukas were excellent swimmers, but they'd never been under a waterfall this strong before. They held their breaths, stayed calm, and grabbed onto the rocks to help climb out.

Don't mind me.

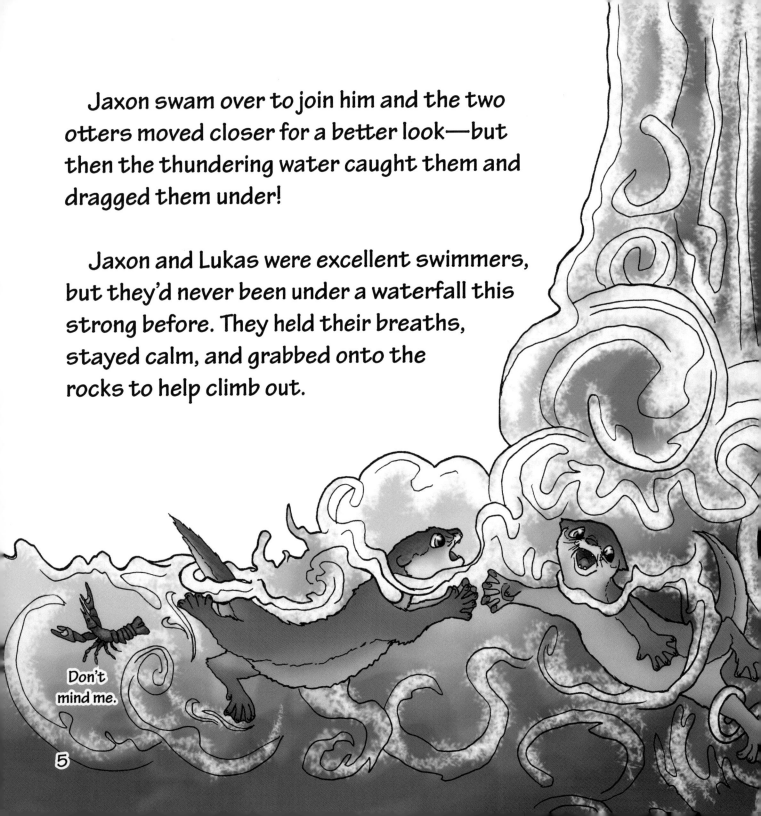

6

They emerged into a cave behind the waterfall. Moss and ferns grew on the walls and even from the ceiling. Light shone in through the waterfall. Jaxon, pointed at something glowing on the floor.

The two otters ran over to look. There was a shining stick and a pearly rock. They reached forward and Lukas picked up the stick while Jaxon picked up the rock. Their hands shook and their fur stood on end.

I think they're magic.

I think you're right. I wonder what they do.

Let's go find out.

8

Lukas put his stick between his jaws, and Jaxon held his rock tight in his teeth. They jumped back into the waterfall and crawled out on the side of the pool. They looked again at what they'd found.

9

Lukas waved his stick through the air, and Jaxon tossed his rock up high and caught it.

How do we make them work?

I don't know. Maybe we have to say magic words.

10

Ha!

Jaxon held his rock out, screwed up his face in concentration, and shouted some "magic" words, but nothing happened. Lukas tried it, too, but couldn't make magic either.

Gobble-dee-gooble-dee-goo!
Make my brother blue!

Hey!

It didn't work anyway.

Well, wobble-dee-flobble-dee-dall! Make my brother small!

I'm already small.

I think it'll take some practice.

Yeah, we'll keep practicing. And then we'll be the most magical magicians ever.

The two boys lifted their stick and rock high and shouted with zeal.

I know rocks and sticks, but I've never seen magic ones.

12

Hey! Those are mine!

Another voice
suddenly shouted with anger,
and the boys jumped in surprise.
Clinging to a branch above them was
a big, grumpy-looking raccoon.

Oh, pardon us, we didn't know they belonged to anyone.

The two otters looked sadly at each other. They'd already start-ed to like their new magic tools. The raccoon scam-pered down the tree and stood before the boys.

13

The raccoon demanded the boys
return the rock and stick.

Now give
them back.

Okay, but will you tell us
how they work?

Yeah. How do you make
magic with them?

But, we felt it when
we picked them up:
magic.

Magic? They aren't
magic; they're just
mine. Now hand
them over.

Oh really? Then
show me this
magic you say
you saw.

14

We tried, but we couldn't make them do anything.

And what did you try to do?

I tried to turn him blue, and he tried to shrink me.

Well, of course that wouldn't work. Magic doesn't work for petty wishes like that.

What does it work for?

Magic is only for your most heart-felt desires, and like all things it has a cost. For every spell you cast, some of your fur will turn white. When you are all white, all the magic you ever had will be gone.

That doesn't seem too bad.

Yeah, it could be way worse!

16

Fine. Take the stick and the rock, then, and when you're done using magic, bring them back here and put them back where you found them.

We will! We promise.

The otters took the stick and rock back with one hand and reached out to shake the paws of the raccoon with the other They ran off with their new magical gifts, and the raccoon watched them go.

18

The boys sped through the forest, each thinking about what his first magic spell would be. They knew now that it had to be something really important. Magic wouldn't work for petty things like shrinking your brother or turning him blue. They thought about things that were more important, but no matter how much they tried to use magic to collect flowers for their mother or to catch fish for their father, they couldn't make magic.

What's he doing?

No idea, Dear.

For many days the otter twins took out their special gifts and tried to make magic in the forest and rivers around their home.

They thought hard about what might be important, but every day they came home with nothing more than dirty paws, a rock, and a stick.

Then one night, there was a terrible storm. The otter family huddled together in their den by the river and tried to sleep. Early in the morning, Lukas woke up because his feet were wet, and he shouted to wake everyone up.

We're being flooded!

The water is too strong to swim in. We can't get out the door. We're trapped.

I'll help us escape!

21

Jaxon ran to the back of the den with his magic rock seized in both hands. He began to glow as he arched back and then slammed the rock into the ceiling. There was a flash of light, and dirt went flying as Jaxon blasted a hole up through the ground.

Lukas lay on the ground above and stuck his stick down into the hole, and the others took hold of the end of it.

Mom, Dad, Jaxon, grab on.

24

Lukas began to glow and, with a great heave, he pulled his family up through the hole and sent them flying.

25

It was still storming, so Gregg suggested they go stay with Mister and Missus Badger: family friends that lived up on a hill, away from the river.

26

Together the family ran through the pouring rain until they reached the badger den. Mister Badger was standing at the entrance with a lamp, looking for them.

At last! There you are.

Badgers are terrific diggers, and Mister Badger had just been thinking he should go check on the Otter family. He could dig into the den if they were trapped inside by a flood.

27

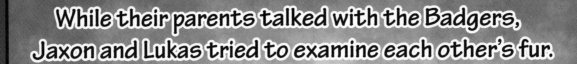

While their parents talked with the Badgers, Jaxon and Lukas tried to examine each other's fur.

Do you see any white spots?

I can't find any, but we did magic!

Yeah, we did!

Maybe the white won't show up for a while.

Maybe we have to do more magic first.

29

The End

This book would not have been possible
without the support of my Kickstarter backers:

Thank You!

Luke Keppler

David Howard

Gregg and Valerie Smith

Jessica Oviedo

Marcella Keppler

Satu

Kathy Roper

The T-Hs

Jason Ken Jones

Russ and Helen Smith

Afton Moman

Ariana Harper Hoke

Keegan & Kennedy Clark

Eagleton Family

Ginny Rorby

Leslie Lajewski

Nick Travis

Nancy Doll

Conor & Owen

Tracy Carlson

(listed in order of time backed)

There are many Northern California animals hidden on these pages. Did you find them all?

River Otter, North American Badger, Western Gray Squirrel, North American Raccoon, Broad-footed Mole, Black Swift, American Dipper, Scrub Jay, American Goldfinch, Marsh Wren, Belted Kingfisher, Allen's Hummingbird, Rough-skinned Newt, Pacific Giant Salamander, Pacific Tree Frog, Rainbow Trout, Flag Crayfish, Broad-banded Forest Snail, Alfalfa Looper Moth, Common Whitetail Dragonfly, California Dancer Damselfly

CPSIA information can be obtained at www.ICGtesting.com
Printed in the USA
LVIW01n0557270116
472444LV00004B/5